Moonshine Cabin

a novella by

Ron Fritsch

ISBN: 979-8985072679

Published by Asymmetric Worlds

For information, address ronfritsch@ronfritsch.com

Front cover art: aimintang

For Lee Ann, my family and the memory of David

The Characters

Annette Hauser, Marilyn and Reed Hauser's mother

Ben Hauser, Marilyn and Reed Hauser's father, a farmer

Marilyn Hauser, Reed Hauser's sister

Reed Hauser, Ethan Tull's best friend

Ethan Tull, Reed Hauser's best friend

Isaac Tull, Ethan Tull's father, a minister

Ruth Tull, Ethan Tull's mother

Chapter One

1954

In the summer between our freshman and sophomore years in high school, Ethan Tull moved with his family to the village of Meadowlark.

We were both 15 years old. He was the only child of Isaac and Ruth Tull. His father was the new minister at the Meadowlark Church, a nondenominational house of worship governed by a board of directors, all of them wealthy, land-owning farmers. Meadowlark was in northern Illinois west of Aurora and south of DeKalb.

My parents, Ben and Annette Hauser, and my sister Marilyn, a year younger than me, sometimes attended the Sunday services at the Meadowlark Church. It was the only church in Meadowlark township.

When I'd turned 14 the previous year, I told my family I'd no longer attend church with them. I knew my parents wouldn't try to change my mind. They owned a King James Version of the Bible and had written my and my sister's names and birth dates inside its front cover, but they'd never read any of it.

Many of the people living in Meadowlark township attended the Congregational church in a village five miles away. They drove that distance, they said, because the minister at the Meadowlark Church, the Reverend Isaac Tull's predecessor, was too extreme in his preaching.

They assumed the new minister, Ethan's father, would be no different. That, they said, was the kind of minister the board wanted.

I'd noticed my parents hadn't seemed to pay much attention to what the previous minister said in his sermons. They sometimes slept, even when he became loud, as he often did.

I once asked my father and mother why they attended church at all. They told me they didn't want people to think we were atheists.

They cited the sad case of the supposedly atheist family of the man who'd most recently rented our cattle-feeding farm. He'd lost his favorable *on shares* lease with the owner. Under such a lease, the landowner and the farmer equally shared the farm's expenses and income. They suffered the bad years, and celebrated the good, together.

The farmer lost the lease, our neighbors told my parents, because he'd spent too much of his time in the Meadowlark Tavern, not far down the street from the church. As a result, his family couldn't go to any church on Sunday. They had no money for the collection plate.

Reverend Tull's predecessor had been asked to leave the church. He'd begun an affair with the woman who'd led the choir. Her husband, who lived with her and their two daughters in the village, had inherited an entire section, 640 acres, in the township. He rented it out to four rent-paying tenants on 160-acre hog farms.

When the cuckold learned of his wife's affair, he confronted the minister on the front porch of the parsonage, which was across the street from the church. His rage was so intense, the neighbors revealed, he saw fit to land several blows with his fist to his adversary's head.

Temporary ministers, most of them retired, filled in for the adulterer until Ethan's father moved to Meadowlark with Ruth and Ethan.

1954

Because I'd chosen not to attend church and I seldom visited the village during the field-work-filled summertime, Ethan and I met on the first day of school, which was the day after Labor Day. Very soon, we could both tell the other took learning seriously. He read, as I did, all of our new textbooks to their end within days after we received them.

We followed important stories in the newspapers and on the television news programs. The U.S. Senate's Army-McCarthy hearings, the French defeat in Vietnam, and the U.S. Supreme Court's decision ruling public school segregation unconstitutional in Brown versus Board of Education were among those we paid attention to that year.

Moonshine Cabin

We called one another to discuss such matters. Whenever my sister heard me speaking with Ethan on our telephone in the kitchen, she rolled her eyes. She'd already informed me he and I were weird.

But she also let me know she wished she had a boyfriend as cute, smart and pleasant as Ethan.

"Then," she said, "I'd simply wait until he and I were old enough to get married, begin our family and live happily ever after."

Marilyn and I were washing and drying the supper dishes, as we always did.

It was my turn to roll my eyes and shake my head as well. "I don't think Ethan and I will ever get married and start a family."

"I hope not," Marilyn said. "I want *him* for myself."

1954

During the first weeks of our sophomore year, Ethan and I decided we'd spend every recess, lunch hour and gym class together.

The brawny boys who enjoyed picking on serious boys like ourselves hadn't caused any trouble for me. I'd already grown to what I assumed would be my size as an adult. I was five foot ten, the same height as my father, and I weighed almost as much as he did too.

I worried about Ethan, though. He was at least two inches shorter than me and slender. But with me at his side, any would-be troublemakers could see starting a fight with either of us would inevitably and immediately start a fight with both of us. And it would no doubt be a fight they'd lose.

My mother, father and Marilyn readily agreed my friendship with Ethan made good sense for both of us. Reverend Isaac Tull, though, insisted we should face, on our own, any bully boys who enjoyed starting fights they had good reasons to think they'd win.

"All you have to do," he said, "is believe in Jesus. If your belief is sincere, I can promise you he'll protect you against any antagonist you might face."

Ethan and his father and I were conversing in the parsonage living room. Ethan and I sat on the sofa. Reverend Tull sat in the stuffed chair he wouldn't let anybody else use.

He was a thin man who'd lost whatever musculature his body might've had in his youth. His face was afflicted with the pallor of those who strictly limit their time spent outdoors.

"God never meant," he continued, "for boys to be close friends. A boy, and later when he becomes a man, needs to make it through his life on earth by himself, on his own. If he can't do that, he becomes Satan's servant, falls into hell when he dies and burns for eternity."

That kind of talk had driven me away from the church.

"If Jesus protects good Christians," I dared to ask, "why did so many of them die in Korea, the last world war and all those other wars this country has fought?"

A number of Christians who'd died in those wars had been members of the Meadowlark Church with exemplary attendance records for the Sunday services. Their names, listed under the names of the wars they'd died in, were engraved on brass plaques on the walls of the rooms the Sunday school classes met in.

"Maybe," Reverend Tull replied to my question, "they weren't, in their hearts, good Christians. We can't question what God does, especially when it comes to death."

I could see Ethan's mother in the kitchen silently shaking her head. Ethan had told me she'd said, on several occasions, even when his father was present, she was glad Ethan and I were such close friends.

The previous minister and his wife had spent a great deal of their time creating a garden in the parsonage backyard. Some people claimed it rivaled Eden. I assumed Ruth Tull owed her robust body and light brown skin to her and Ethan's efforts to keep the parsonage backyard fit to be compared to the home of Adam and Eve in their innocence.

1954

Moonshine Cabin

In the mornings I'd take the bus to school with Marilyn. Often, though, on my way home on pleasant-weather days, I'd walk with Ethan to the parsonage. We'd do our homework together in his bedroom.

When we were done, I'd walk, or run, the two miles, via the gravel roads, to my family's farm and arrive in time to feed the cattle their ground corn and cobs and their hay, eat supper with my family and help my sister with the dishes afterward.

For us to have more time together, Ethan would walk, or run, half the distance with me before he'd turn around and walk, or run, a second mile back to the parsonage, like me then, alone.

1954

Soon after Ethan and I had begun doing our homework in the parsonage, his father came into Ethan's room one afternoon when I was there. Without a word to explain what he was up to, he began unscrewing the bolts that held the inside lock on the door and the wall next to the door.

"Now you know, Ethan," he said when he was done, "I'll be free to walk in here anytime I please. You and your atheist friend won't hide your wickedness from me."

Ethan shook his head. "We're not engaged in any wickedness in here. Unless you think doing homework is wicked."

"Then you won't mind," Reverend Tull said, "my removing the inside lock on your door."

"I don't mind at all," Ethan said. "Walk in here anytime you please—if you have nothing better to do."

1955

Ethan's father didn't stop there. In the latter half of our sophomore year, he saw fit to put an end to our homework arrangement.

After school one day, as Ethan and I approached the parsonage, Reverend Tull stood at the top of the stairs to the front porch.

"You're no longer welcome in this house," he told me when we reached the stairs.

"Wait a minute," Ethan said. "Why is Reed no longer welcome in this house? He's my best friend. We like to study together. Schoolwork is a lot more fun that way."

Reverend Tull turned to his son.

"Frankly," he said, "I find your close friendship with this snotty atheist boy appalling. Nothing good can ever come from it."

I wasn't an atheist. I doubted, though, there was a god, never seen and never heard by humans, who somehow ruled the world. I also assumed the Christian story was something people had made up and continued to believe, like Ethan, because it gave them hope an earthly death didn't mean they'd cease to exist.

I only knew for certain I had a life to live on a planet called earth orbiting a star known as the sun, and I wanted to make the most of it.

Ethan had asked me why I didn't attend church with my family if I wasn't an atheist.

"I'll tell you why," I said. "I don't like the hypocrisy."

"What hypocrisy?"

"A good example of it," I said, "was that man who was the minister here before your father, the guy they kicked out because he was having an affair with the choir director. He taught the Sunday school class for teenage boys. He told us playing with ourselves with our hands was a terrible sin, and we should never do it, no matter how good we might think it felt. He insisted sex was something men and women only did with their legal spouses. He told us that at the same time he was having an affair with a woman who was another person's spouse."

Ethan laughed. "My father teaches that class now. He also tells us playing with ourselves is one of the worst sins imaginable."

"And you don't believe it."

"Of course not."

Moonshine Cabin

"And you do it too."

Ethan laughed again. "As often as I can. Don't you?"

"Hell, yes, I do. At least once every day."

Chapter Two

1955

Ethan's mother stepped through the front doorway of the parsonage and onto the porch and, this time, gave voice to her disagreement with Reverend Tull.

"I see nothing at all wrong with Ethan's friendship with Reed," she said. "It's as if they're brothers."

"Ethan doesn't need a brother," his father said. "He has Jesus."

Ethan's mother shook her head. "Jesus never said people can't want the friendship of other people on this earth. He never said two 16-year-old boys can't be best friends."

"Nevertheless," Ethan's father said, looking at me, "you'll never set foot inside this house again. If you do, I'll have the sheriff's deputy remove you and take you to a reformatory for delinquent boys, where you belong."

The county sheriff's deputy he referred to lived in Meadowlark. He was the only law enforcement officer the township had.

Ethan's mother shook her head again but said nothing more.

I said my good-byes to her and Ethan and ran home.

Why, I wondered, did Reverend Tull believe I belonged in a reformatory for delinquent boys? Did he think I was queer? Did he imagine I wanted to have sex with Ethan?

As I neared my family's farm, an idea popped up in my head.

1955

At the end of the next day at school, I told Ethan I wanted to show him something. I took him down an alley to the southern edge of the village.

A woven-wire fence topped with two strands of barbed wire stood between us and a woods. Behind a broken-down shed, we came to a wooden gate bearing a "Keep Out Private Property" sign.

Moonshine Cabin

Beyond the gate, a dirt path began.

Ethan helped me slide the gate open.

"I didn't know," he said, "there was a gate here. Where does the path go?"

"Come on, you'll find out."

We closed the gate behind us and began walking on the path in a southwesterly direction into the springtime woods.

As we walked, I began to think Ethan's father might've done us a favor in refusing to let us do our homework in the parsonage any longer.

Marilyn was right. Ethan was a good-looking guy. I preferred his brown eyes and hair to my blue eyes and blond hair. I didn't think I was queer, but I did want to be with him as much as I could.

We approached some cattle grazing in a sunny, grassy area near the path. We stopped to take a look.

"Whose cows are these?" Ethan asked.

I laughed. "Look more closely. They're not cows."

"What are they?"

"They're steers and heifers," I said. "The steers had their balls cut off shortly after they were born. They'll never be bulls. The heifers will never have calves. They belong to my family and our landlady. This is my family's farm. These cattle are the way we make a living."

"How do you do that?"

"We buy calves shipped in from the west, feed them a lot of corn and hay to adulthood, and pay a trucker to take them to the stockyards in Chicago. That's where we sell them. They become damned tasty steaks, roasts, ribs and burgers."

We reached a one-story log cabin with a sturdy brick chimney at one end of it. It didn't appear to serve any present purpose.

"This," I said, "is what I wanted you to see."

The southernmost end of the woods we were in was behind the house my family occupied, our cattle barn and our corncrib. The flat land we raised our crops on lay further south, across a gravel road.

The woods sloped down from our farmyard to the Meadowlark Creek, which flowed through the property west to east on its way to the Fox, Illinois and Mississippi rivers. The woods sloped upward on the northern side of the stream.

The dirt path Ethan and I had been on continued across the valley to the farmyard. Using it sometimes required a walk through the creek with boots on.

Usually, though, the water was low enough to allow a crossing on a line of flat rocks. Marilyn and I, in between our many Monopoly games, had placed them where they were for that purpose.

1955

I told Ethan why my family had a log cabin surrounded by wild violets and bleeding hearts blooming in our woods.

During the 1920s, the farmer who owned and worked the 200-acre property discovered he could earn more money distilling and selling moonshine to the local speakeasies than he could feeding and selling livestock at the stockyards in Chicago.

He built the cabin to enclose his still. The logs he used to construct the walls were formerly the limbs of oak trees. He used cement blocks for the foundation. The cabin had no basement.

During the night the farmer-moonshiner used the path to go northeast to Meadowlark to make deliveries to the buyers. His two horses pulled a wagon loaded with barrels of his whiskey through the rear entrance of the shed he'd rented at the end of the path. While the townspeople slept, he and his customers, who used the front entrance, quietly transferred the barrels from his wagon to their trucks.

Despite the farmer's efforts to keep his criminal business a secret, Al Capone's people used threats and physical force to obtain, from at least one of the speakeasy owners, the identity of their moonshine supplier. The gang passed that information on to the authorities who enforced—as well, or not, as they could—the Prohibition laws.

The hapless moonshiner-farmer went to prison. His former customers began working for Capone.

The authorities seized and auctioned off his farm to a doctor and his wife. They resided on the west side of the Fox River in Aurora, which was where the wealthier residents of that city lived.

After the doctor and his wife died, they left the farm to their daughter, their only child. Never married, she'd lived with and cared for them to the end of their lives.

The daughter took into her home—as a live-in maid, her family and neighbors assumed—another unmarried woman. The doctor's daughter became my family's landlady soon after I was born in 1939.

1955

My mother and father had grown up in and near a village similar to Meadowlark but east of Rockford. My mother's parents owned the bank. My father's parents paid cash rent for an 80-acre dairy farm.

In the late 1930s, my mother's parents decided she should marry the son of the owners of a bank in a neighboring town. They hoped to merge the families as well as the banks. Both banks had so far survived the Great Depression and should, both families believed, move on to greater glory and wealth for them all.

On the other hand, my mother had decided she was in love with a strapping high-school classmate, Ben Hauser, who was equally in love with her. Her mother and father told her there was only one word for a young woman in a well-to-do family who'd rather marry a dirt-poor farmer for love than the young man her parents had chosen for her to enhance the position of her family. That word was *whore*.

Annette's family warned her. If she married Ben Hauser, they'd disown her. Her brother, her only sibling, would inherit the bank and everything else her family owned. My mother would receive nothing.

Nor would they include her, Ben or their children in any family activities. They'd disown them all.

When my mother and father graduated from high school in 1938, they told their families she had no choice but to break her engagement to the bankers' son, and they also had no choice but to marry each other.

Annette was pregnant. Ben had to be the child's father. He was the only person she'd ever been intimate with. I was their love child.

Her family kept their promise to have nothing further to do with her. They told her the day she married Ben would be the last day she could set foot inside their house.

My father's family felt they had no choice but to likewise disown him and his offspring. My mother's parents owned their farm.

My father's older brother and his wife, as well as my father's older sister and her husband, were cash-paying tenants on two of my mother's parents'other 80-acre dairy farms in the half-section they owned. They would've rented their fourth 80-acre dairy farm to my father—if he hadn't married Annette.

My father found a job as a hired man on a large cattle farm near Aurora. One of the wealthiest families in Chicago owned it. They paid my father a pittance for his hard work, but they provided him and my mother a modest frame house to live in rent-free. It had indoor plumbing, a feature the 80-acre dairy farm he grew up on lacked.

I was born in that house. My parents hadn't enough money to pay for my mother to give birth to me in a hospital.

The only relative I'd ever met was my father's paternal aunt. She was the single woman living with the doctor's daughter in Aurora who'd inherited a 200-acre farm with a woods in Meadowlark township.

My father's aunt thought it a shame her hard-working nephew was a poorly paid hired man. He would've graduated from high school as the valedictorian of his class if my mother hadn't won that honor.

Soon after my birth in February 1939, the doctor's daughter evicted her booze-loving tenant and leased the property to my family as her father had leased it to his tenant farmers.

Moonshine Cabin

She split with us, 50-50, the expenses of the farm as well as the income.

She and my father's aunt often came to see us. Whenever they did, my mother gave them a chicken or two she'd beheaded and butchered, at least a dozen freshly laid eggs, vegetables from our garden and fruit Marilyn and I had picked in the orchard and vineyard.

During World War II my mother and father dipped into their savings to buy a camera. Every Christmas after that, they sent pictures of Marilyn and me to our maternal and paternal grandparents. They included notes on our growth, education and similar matters, even on our surviving measles, mumps and whooping cough.

My mother and father were still doing it. In all those years, they'd never received a response to their holiday missives, not even a thank-you note. Resentment, Marilyn and I had learned, died hard.

1955

I'd brought with me the two keys my family had for the cabin door. Despite the rust on the key and the lock, I was able to open the door the first time I tried.

Ethan and I entered the cabin. The only pieces of furniture in it were a square wooden table and two wooden chairs. The moonshiner's plank floor was dusty but still in good condition.

I slid away the pieces of wood covering the window openings on the north and south walls. The window screens were old and rusty, but they could still keep mosquitoes and other woodland insects out of a cabin they might've otherwise chosen to visit.

The authorities had removed the equipment the moonshiner had used to make his product, but the brick hearth beneath the chimney looked as if it could support a fire to warm the cabin and provide some light on a cold and dark winter day, maybe even during a cold and dark winter night.

19

"We can do our homework here," I said. "What more do we need than a table and two chairs?"

Chapter Three

1955

I looked at Ethan. "This is what I wanted you to see. We can easily walk here after school. This is about halfway between your parsonage in Meadowlark and my family's house."

"That's great," Ethan said. "You're right. This is the perfect place to do our homework."

"I knew you'd think so."

Ethan looked at me. "You figured this out. You and I'll be alone here. I'll tell my parents I'm doing my homework at your place. I won't need to tell my father about this cabin."

"Your father shouldn't object. My family always coughs up some hard-earned money when the collection plate comes around to them on Sunday mornings."

Ethan snickered. "He pays close attention to that sort of thing."

"And you'll be telling your parents the truth. I'll let my family know what we're doing. It'll make good sense to them."

"They won't mind we're in this cabin in the woods together? With nobody around to watch over us?"

I shook my head. "We're 16. They like you, much more than they do your father. They're glad you're my friend. They won't have a problem with us being together in this moonshine cabin."

"I'll bring our chess board and pieces to school tomorrow. Then we can keep them here and play a game whenever we want."

Ethan and I had ordered the chess set from a Sears catalogue, splitting the cost.

I gave him one of the two keys for the door lock.

After Ethan left, I went home and got some rags to dust off the table and chairs and an old broom to sweep the floor. I also brought two Mason jars my mother said I could have.

Since the farmer-moonshiner needed water for his new business, he'd had a well drilled near the cabin. The hand pump the well diggers had installed still worked. Ethan and I would have fresh, cold water whenever we wanted it.

Beginning the next afternoon, Ethan and I did our homework in our moonshine cabin in the woods.

1955

Every day after Ethan and I had admitted we willfully violated the rule against playing with ourselves, we goaded one another into revealing when and where we'd done it the previous day. Both of us found answering the question less and less embarrassing.

We mostly committed the sin under the covers in our beds when, if we'd been obedient 16-year-old Christians, we would've been sleeping, or desperately attempting to.

One warm, sunny day in June soon after we'd finished our sophomore year, Ethan came up with a plan to change our routine.

"We could do it here," he said, "in our moonshine cabin."

"Together?" I asked. "In front of one another?"

"Why not? Neither of us has anything to hide from his best friend in the world."

"No, I guess we don't."

We'd seen one another without any clothes on before and after every gym class. We had adjoining lockers in the shower room. We always took our showers together.

With nothing further to discuss, we performed an act we hadn't previously achieved with another person's eyes upon us. Neither he nor I seemed at all bothered by it.

Ethan and I came to realize we'd achieved freedom to an extent we hadn't previously imagined possible. We never could've done in his bedroom in the parsonage, with the inside door lock removed, what we did in our cabin.

After that, neither of us wanted to violate Reverend Tull's rule except when we were in the presence of the other, and that was always in the cabin. We even promised one another we'd only do it if we were together.

1955

After I ate supper with my family one evening and washed and dried the dishes with Marilyn, I took to the cabin two old quilt blankets my mother had said I could have. I laid them on the floor, one on top of the other.

Ethan laughed when he saw them the next day. "These are just what we need. We can lie together."

The previous week, Ethan's father had left him a hand-written Old Testament quotation on his bed. Ethan had brought it to the cabin.

"Thou shalt not lie with mankind as with womankind," the note said. "It is an abomination."

Reverend Isaac Tull had underlined *not*, *mankind* and *abomination*.

Ethan had chosen not to speak with his father about the note.

Lying on the blankets later that afternoon, Ethan and I turned to one another and closed the distance between us.

Previously, we'd always pulled back at that point. This time, we didn't. Our lips came together. We kissed.

I'd admitted to myself I wanted to kiss Ethan on his lips.

He'd apparently wanted to kiss me as much as I did him.

When we took a break, several minutes later, Ethan had a question for me. "Does this mean my father's right? We're queer?"

I shrugged my shoulders. "Maybe we are queer. It doesn't matter to me anymore. I love you. That's all that matters as far as I'm concerned."

Ethan nodded. "And I love you."

"I know you do. And if our loving one another makes us queer, I'm all for it."

"Me too."

We decided to kiss some more, even as we knew we could very well become addicted to it. It could also lead us to engage in other forbidden activities. By then, I was fervently hoping it would.

1955

Ethan and I were three weeks into our junior year in high school. The goldenrods were in full bloom all along the path when I walked home from my latest lying-with-mankind session on the quilts with him.

It was time for my evening chores. I fed the hungry cattle, now in their barn, their pails of ground corn and cobs and their bales of hay.

After I finished my work, I entered the house through the back door, as I usually did. I found Ethan's father sitting at our round kitchen table with my parents and sister. He didn't know it, but he occupied the chair I sat on whenever my family ate a meal.

He glared at me. "Where's my son?" he asked.

"He should be home by now," I said. "If you have any doubt about it, why don't you call and find out for yourself? I'm certain my parents will let you use our telephone to do it."

My reply failed to mollify Reverend Tull.

"Your mother and father," he said, "tell me he was probably with you in a log cabin in your woods. I'd never heard about this cabin before. I wonder why Ethan never felt any need to say anything about it to me, his father."

Ethan had told his mother all about our moonshine cabin.

I hadn't asked my parents or sister to lie about the visits Ethan and I made to the cabin.

"Ethan and I were in the cabin," I said. "As we often do, we walked to it after school. We do our homework there."

Reverend Tull sneered. "What else do you and my son do in that cabin?"

"Sometimes we play a game of chess. That didn't happen today. We had too much homework to do."

24

Moonshine Cabin

Ethan's father scoffed. "Why am I supposed to believe what you're telling me?"

My parents and Marilyn seemed surprised by the harsh tone of Reverend Tull's questioning.

I shook my head. "I don't give a good goddamn whether *you* believe me or not."

I watched Ethan's father blink his eyes at me, and I had to laugh.

"I'm sure my mother and father and sister believe me," I said. "They're the only persons present whose opinions matter to me."

Reverend Tull turned to my father. "Doesn't it concern you and Mrs. Hauser two 16-year-old boys spend so much time together? And alone, in a cabin, hidden in the woods?"

"The cabin isn't hidden in the woods," I said. "It's on a dirt path that goes from behind our barn all the the way to Meadowlark, thanks to the moonshiner who laid it down. He used it for his deliveries to his customers during Prohibition."

Marilyn laughed. She'd enjoyed our landlady's moonshiner story as much as I had.

My mother turned to Ethan's father. "I think it's admirable two 16-year-old boys take their homework so seriously they help one another with it. I understand your son gets good grades on his report card, the same as Reed and Marilyn do."

Reverend Tull glared at my mother.

She wasn't done. "If they also find the time to play a game of chess, I don't see anything wrong with that. Your wife told me chess is good for a person's brain. Maybe I should take it up. Maybe I should ask Ethan and Reed to teach me how to play it. Or would you have us believe Jesus doesn't look kindly on people playing a game like that? It's too much like playing cards and dancing?"

Once again, Reverend Tull sneered. "Your son and my son spend far too much time together. I suspect there's something going on between them they're not telling us about, something they know they're not supposed to be doing."

25

I also sneered. "What you're saying is all in your filthy mind. It has nothing to do with reality. It's all in your filthy, demented mind. I wouldn't say it's even slightly Christian."

My father shook his head. "I'm afraid you've crossed a line, Reverend Tull. You're accusing our son of some mysterious misbehavior. But we have no reason in the world to believe he and your son are doing anything wrong, whether they're in that cabin or anywhere else they want to be."

"Ethan and Reed," my mother said, "are both well-behaved boys. They never get into fights with the other boys. Their teachers like them, even praise them. I'm not going to sit here and listen to you accuse them of anything."

My father rose to his feet and stared down at Ethan's father. "I believe, sir, the time has come for you to leave this house. We've heard enough of your whining insinuations."

My mother and sister also rose to their feet.

I hadn't sat down since I came through the back door. I still had the books I'd brought home from school in my backpack. I'd do my homework in my room before I went to bed that evening.

Ethan's father shook his head. "You're going to let this atheist boy have his way?"

My mother answered that question. "He's free to believe whatever he wishes. As long as it doesn't hurt anybody else."

Reverend Tull wasn't ready to give up. He remained seated in my chair at my family's round oaken table.

"And you'll throw your pastor out of your house?" he asked.

My mother laughed. "If a pastor comes into our house spreading vicious lies about our son, we'll gladly ask the asshole to leave. And we'll specifically warn him to never come back again."

As my parents, Marilyn and I hovered over Reverend Tull, he stared at me. "You'll spend eternity in hell," he said. "You'll discover God doesn't tolerate your misbehavior."

Chapter Four

1955

My father worked his way around the table until he stood behind the pastor. He bent over enough to wrap his arms around him under his armpits, lift him to his feet and walk him to the door to our back porch.

Marilyn helpfully opened the door.

My father shoved the pastor through the doorway so forcibly he fell to his knees on the porch.

Marilyn closed the door.

We watched through the two windows in the wall between the kitchen and the back porch.

The pastor lifted himself up to his feet again and staggered to his 1938 Chevrolet in our driveway. He seated himself in it, backed it onto the road and drove it east toward Meadowlark.

I called Ethan and let him know what had happened.

He told me he'd barricade himself in his room. He'd done it before. He said his mother would bring him his supper.

Marilyn and I prepared beef liver and onions for our supper. That was a meal we all favored. The onions came from our garden.

We'd recently taken a steer to the butcher. We always split the meat with our landlady. The liver was the first thing we ate.

1955

During lunch the next day at school, Ethan told me he and his father had had a loud argument at the breakfast table that morning.

His father told him he wouldn't permit him to visit the cabin again.

"I'm quite certain," his father said, "you and that nasty Reed Hauser are up to no good in your cabin."

"Do you intend to obey your father?" I asked.

Ethan laughed. "Hell, no. I'll visit you in the cabin as damned often as I please, which is as often as you want me there."

"You'll defy your parents?"

"I'll defy one of my parents, my father. My mother said she wasn't opposed to our meeting in the cabin."

Ethan finished eating his sandwich.

"My mother went on to say, as she always does, she's quite certain you're a good friend for me to have. She said you're very well behaved and like to study."

"Did your father accept that?"

"No, he told my mother she'll soon realize how deluded she is about you. But what can he do? As long as my mother says I can go to the cabin with you, I'll do it. Beginning this afternoon. My mother isn't going to change her mind just because my father thinks she should."

I nodded. "Good for her."

"He'll just have to get over it. I don't know why he's so concerned about what we do in the cabin anyway. We aren't hurting anybody else. That bible of his has a lot of rules most people don't pay any attention to. Like all those things we're not supposed to eat."

1955

Reverend Tull was waiting for Ethan in his 1938 Chevrolet outside the school that afternoon.

"Get in this car, Ethan," his father said. "I'm taking you home."

Ethan kept walking with me. We were on our way to our cabin in the woods.

"I'll be home later," he said to his father. "I'm doing my homework with Ethan first. We've found us a very quiet, peaceful place to do it."

Reverend Tull drove off by himself.

A number of students had heard Ethan openly defy his father. Some of them attended the Meadowlark Church with their families.

Moonshine Cabin

1955

One cool Saturday afternoon in late October—the hickories and oaks in the woods were in full bloom—Ethan realized his father was following him, at a distance, on the path to the cabin.

I was standing in the warm sunshine near the cabin when Ethan approached.

I laughed. "Why are you in such a hurry?"

Ethan wasn't laughing. "Get ready for my father. He's following me."

Then I saw Reverend Tull trudging toward us. He appeared to be badly out of breath after his long walk from Meadowlark.

"I'm ready for your father," I told Ethan.

As his father drew near, he pointed an index finger toward the cabin. "So this," he asked, "is where you claim to do your homework?"

"What Ethan and I do here," I said, "is no concern of yours."

Reverend Tull looked at me as if I'd delivered a blow to his head. "I'm Ethan's father."

"Nevertheless," I said, "what Ethan and I do in this cabin is no concern of yours. We're 16 years old. We decide what we do in the privacy of our cabin. You have nothing to say about it."

Reverend Tull wasn't done. "Might I look inside?"

He'd see the blankets on the floor.

"You might not," I said. "In fact, you'll leave this property as soon as you can get your tired ass back to that gateway in Meadowlark. You passed through it without any invitation to do so. This is my family's farm. I'm certain you remember my father and mother told you you're not welcome to set foot upon it. The last time you paid us a visit, they tossed you out like the rotten piece of garbage you are."

I paused to let those words sink in.

"And yet here you are again," I said, "trespassing in full violation of the law. And you hold yourself out to be a messenger from heaven informing mere humans as to what's right and what's wrong on

29

this earth. I think you've proved you're not what you want people to think you are. You're an imposter. You have nothing to say to me."

Ethan's father stared at me speechless, perhaps unable to believe I'd possessed the temerity to say what I'd said to a Christian minister.

"So you'll turn around now," I said to him, "walk back the way you came, go through that gateway and never come here again. If you do, my family will ask the deputy sheriff to arrest you for trespass. Maybe some time in jail will make you behave."

Reverend Tull's response was succinct. "You'll end up in the deepest pit in hell."

I laughed.

Then he turned to Ethan. "And so will you if you don't separate yourself from this Christ-rejecting wretch."

Ethan laughed. "I have absolutely no wish to do that."

Once again, Reverend Tull looked as if he'd taken a blow to his head.

Ethan wasn't done. "Reed Hauser is the best friend I've ever had. Now do as he tells you and get your goddamned ass off his family's property."

His father turned and began plodding through the autumn leaves on the path back to Meadowlark.

If I'd seen him without knowing who he was, I would've felt sorry for him.

Ethan and I followed him far enough to watch him close the gate behind him.

1955

That same day Ethan and I figured out how to keep the window sliders open enough to let a good breeze pass through the cabin even as they prevented any peeping Isaac from seeing us if we remained within 15 feet of the fireplace. That was where we had the blankets spread out on the floor anyway.

Moonshine Cabin

I looked at the old door lock and shook my head.

"I'm afraid," I said, "it's too old, rusty and small to keep out anybody determined to get inside this cabin. We need something to keep intruders out at least when we're in here. But don't worry, I'll see what I can find to do that."

The next day I rummaged through my father's toolshed and found a pair of rusty but still sturdy U-shaped steel clasps I was certain I'd seen there before. In the pile of leftover lumber we'd saved, I found a two-by-four long enough to do what I wanted it to do. I also located some sturdy steel bolts for the clasps.

Using my father's biggest screwdriver, Ethan and I bolted one clasp to the logs inside the cabin close to the door and the other clasp to the inner side of the door itself. We could insert the two-by-four into the steel clasps whenever we were in the cabin and wanted to bar entry to it by Reverend Isaac Tull or any other wandering snoop who might want to discover what we were doing in our lair.

After we finished the construction work, we could only sit naked on my mother's blankets with our arms around each other and marvel at what we'd done with our cabin. In it, we could seal ourselves off from the world.

1955

Later that afternoon, Ethan had a question for me. "Why is it only my father has accused us of misbehavior in this cabin? Nobody else says anything about what we do, or don't do, here."

I shrugged. "I don't think anybody else wants to confront what we might be doing."

"You think other people maybe wonder if we're doing queer things in our cabin?"

"I suspect your mother and my mother and father and sister have probably wondered if we're sexually involved. We can't deny we're healthy, horny teenagers. I doubt the truth would surprise them."

31

"My mother has never said anything about it to me. Has your mother, father or sister said anything about it to you?"

I shook my head. "That's why I think they'd rather not confront the question. Your mother too. As long as we don't say anything about it, and we keep ourselves hidden here when we do queer things, they also won't say anything about it. But they almost have to wonder. We spend so much time together. We're not dating our female classmates. Everything we do socially, we do together."

Ethan laughed. "We don't go to church together."

I laughed too. "That's the only exception we make."

"What about other people around here? Do you think they wonder about us?"

"I wouldn't be surprised if they do. I'd guess by now most of the people who know us know we've got this cabin in the woods. Wondering why we spend so much time in it together would seem natural."

"But they never say anything about it."

I shrugged again. "Like your mother and my mother and father and sister, they probably don't want to deal with it. And that's a good thing for us. As long as we do what we do within the four walls of this cabin and never say anything about it, they'll let us get away with doing something we're not supposed to do—lying with mankind on old quilt blankets."

Ethan nodded. "I can only hope you're right."

Chapter Five

1955

Ethan had another question for me. "So why does my father, unlike everybody else who knows us, want to confront us about doing what queers do?"

I shook my head. "I don't know. I can't figure him out. He seemed to know we were queer before we did."

"I thought he was nuts."

"So did I when he removed the lock on your bedroom door. And even more so when he told me I was no longer welcome in the parsonage."

"Yeah. We hadn't even imagined then doing what we do every day now. I guess if you're going to be accused of doing something sinful anyway, you might as well do it, especially if it feels so damned good."

I laughed. "At least your father hasn't made his accusations outside our families. We can be grateful for that."

"Yeah. So you think we've got to keep our mouths shut?"

"We never tell anybody what we do in this cabin. If somebody else accuses us of any kind of misbehavior here, we just deny it. We never admit it. We insist on our right to be left alone."

After thinking a moment, Ethan nodded. "Yeah, that's what we've got to do. And be damned careful nobody can see us in here. We bar the door and keep the window sliders where they need to be."

That became our bedrock agreement. We'd never tell another person what we did when we were alone together.

And as long as we had our moonshine cabin in the woods, with quietly grazing cattle our only neighbors, we'd believe we were as near to bliss as humans living on our earth could ever hope to be.

1955

We realized, though, nothing would stop Reverend Tull.

Almost daily after his hike into the woods, he insisted Ethan quit seeing me in the cabin.

Ethan—and his mother, if she was present—ignored his demands.

"My father can't inflict any punishment on me," Ethan said. "My mother will simply undo it."

I'd wondered about that. "What if he complains to the juvenile authorities about his misbehaving son? What stops him from going that route? Is it because the minister of the Meadowlark Church doesn't want his parishioners finding out he has a wayward son he can't control? I can see why he might not want that."

Ethan laughed. "I forgot to tell you. I called the juvenile authorities. They informed me they won't take any action against me as long as my mother gives me her consent to be your friend. They said it isn't their job to choose between parents in deciding how they raise their children. That's what divorce court judges do, they told me."

"And your mother is still perfectly okay with you coming here to see me, despite your father's adamant opposition?"

"She says I can come here to see you whenever I want, how often I want. She knows I'm as safe with you here as I would be at home. She doesn't blame me for wanting to put some distance between my father and myself. All he and I do anymore is argue about you."

"I'm damned glad to hear your mother is on our side."

"As long as I do well in school and stay out of mischief with the bad boys and girls, my mother says she'll be very happy I have you as my best friend."

Neither Ethan nor I even knew who the bad boys and girls were. He and I were simply pleasant toward all the other students. We suspected many of them had long since placed us high on their lists of the most boring people they'd ever met. And that's just what we wanted.

1956

Moonshine Cabin

One Saturday after a late-winter snowfall during the previous night, Ethan and I spent the afternoon in the cabin. We'd both turned 17. Halfway into our adventure that day, we heard somebody, apparently wearing heavy boots, walking in the slushy snow outside.

"That's my father," Ethan whispered. "He told me he was going to pay another visit to our cabin and put a stop to what I'm doing with you. He knew damned well I'd be here with you this afternoon."

Ethan's father ended up at the door. Without knocking first, he turned the doorknob and pulled on it.

Ethan and I stared at our two-by-four nestled in the clasps we'd bolted to the door and the wall. It wasn't budging. The bolts were holding the steel clasps in place as we'd hoped they would. They resisted Reverend Tull's additional attempts to pull the door open.

"What the fuck!" he yelled, giving voice to his intense frustration.

Ethan and I laughed out loud. Our hard work had paid off.

"Ethan," his father yelled, "I know you're in there with that snotty Reed Hauser. I know what you're doing with him. It's an abomination. I demand you open this door."

Ethan and I were sitting on our blankets as naked as we were the moment our mothers gave birth to us. During the winter we kept the window sliders tightly closed. We had a nice fire going on the hearth.

Ethan and I regularly searched the woods for downed tree limbs. We sawed them and brought the chunks back to the cabin in my father's wheelbarrow. Then we chopped them into smaller pieces with his axe. We currently had a large pile of them stacked outside near the door.

Ethan had let me know he liked the smell of our fires. I told him the hickory and oak wood gave the fires the smell we both liked.

"Ethan," his father yelled again. "I know you're in there. And I want you out. Now."

I wondered if maybe the carefully stacked pile of wood, the smoke rising from the moonshiner's chimney, and the obvious fact that Ethan and I were inside the cabin enjoying the fire had driven Reverend

Isaac Tull into a kind of madness. Something in his world was very wrong—Ethan and I were in love. And there was nothing he could do about it.

Ethan decided to speak up. "Go away," he yelled. "I'm not coming out. We're not opening the door. We're not doing anything wrong."

Ethan's father wasn't about to give up. "I know you're lying, Ethan. I want you out of there. I want to save your soul."

Ethan laughed. "My soul doesn't need saving. But yours does. You're trespassing again. You have no right at all to be present in these woods. Reed's parents made that clear to you. So get out of here. Now. Go. Go away. And don't come back."

"Goddamn you, Ethan!"

I couldn't help but laugh again. "Does your father swear like that very often?"

"He does if he's certain nobody who goes to Meadowlark Church is present and can hear him."

"Don't you go to that church?"

Ethan laughed. "He makes exceptions for Mom and me."

Ethan's father gave voice to several more loud pleas for Ethan to acknowledge how badly he was sinning.

"You've got to change your ways!" Reverend Tull screamed. "Otherwise, you'll end up in hell for eternity!"

Ethan chose not to make another reply. Inside our cabin only the crackling of the fire broke the silence.

After another half hour or so of intermittent yelling, Ethan's father gave up his foolish attempt to break into our hiding place. We could hear him trudging away in the sloppy snow.

Ethan and I had known we could've waited deep into the evening for his father to quit. We had enough wood inside our cabin to take us well past the time we would've opened the door and found Reverend Tull frozen to death.

Moonshine Cabin

But his foolish visit never would've gotten that far. My father would've noticed I hadn't fed the cattle their evening meal. He would've fed them himself and then driven the tractor to the cabin to find out what was wrong.

He would've discovered Ethan's father at the door. He would've asked him to leave the property at once. If Reverend Tull refused to do so, my father would've driven the tractor back to our house, called the deputy sheriff and asked him to escort the trespasser out of the woods and back to Meadowlark.

I wondered if my father would've pressed charges against him. I wondered if a judge would've made him spend some time in jail.

Ethan looked at me and smiled. His father's abject humiliation didn't seem to bother him at all. At times like these, he appeared to enjoy his father's futile quest to save his soul.

If my father had attempted to interfere in my relationship with Ethan, I would've felt myself lost in a universe I could never understand.

Despite our lack of clothing in our warm cabin, Ethan and I hadn't been lying with mankind when his father showed up.

We'd been deeply involved in a chess game. Ethan had come up with a series of clever moves I'd never seen before.

If I didn't soon come up with some clever moves of my own, he was going to win—and I'd have to listen to him crow about his big victory for the next week or more.

1956

In the two years I'd known Ethan, he'd grown a couple of inches and was now my height. We'd begun to understand we'd both reached our adult size.

Our mothers insisted we shave, preferably daily. Neither of them wanted to see hair growing on the faces of their baby boys. They also wanted the hair on the top of our heads short. We were glad to please them. We also liked cleanly shaven faces and crewcuts.

We took gym class as seriously as we did our other classes, even math, chemistry, history and English. Toward the end of our junior year, the football coach asked us to speak with him in his office, privately. When we did, he invited us to join the team.

He told us Ethan could train to become the starting quarterback. And I could hope to become the starting tight end. I'd save Ethan's ass whenever an opponent broke through our offensive line. I'd also be the receiver he could always pass to whenever nobody else was open. Many, many game-winning touchdowns, the coach said, were ours for the asking.

Ethan was slender, but he now had strong legs and arms. He could throw a football farther than the current starting quarterback could. Training would improve his accuracy. He was quick-witted and had great eyesight. He could look down the field after a snap and readily see which receiver was most likely to break open. I didn't say so, but I agreed with the coach. Ethan could've become, in our conference, the game-winning quarterback Meadowlark High School needed.

And I might've become the tight end the coach had in mind. The farm work I'd done, and maybe some genes I'd inherited from my father, had given me the ability to block stronger and bigger players in gym class. I was also a fast and evasive runner when I wanted to be.

Ethan and I thanked the coach for his offer but knew we'd never have the time we'd need to train with the football team.

We'd both decided we'd go the University of Illinois if we could obtain the scholarships we hoped for. Those would require we keep getting an A in every subject on every report card. Not wanting to take any chances, we'd have to spend as many long hours as we could with our noses in our books, preferably in our quiet cabin in the woods.

Chapter Six

1956

Reverend Tull had told Ethan he'd only consider spending his money for him to attend a Christian school like Wheaton College, and then only for the purpose of his becoming a minister.

Ethan bluntly told his father he hadn't the slightest interest in doing that.

His father told him he'd fallen under my influence, like a sinner blatantly choosing Satan for his guide.

Ethan laughed. "Reed Hauser doesn't have anything to do with my not wanting to follow in your footsteps. I decided on that, all by myself, long before I met him."

Ruth Tull had no money of her own to help Ethan go to college. Prior to their marriage, Reverend Tull had laid down a strict rule. A minister's wife couldn't work outside the home. She needed to be the mistress of the parsonage and nothing else.

Ruth had agreed to abide by the rule. She told Ethan her job prospects when she and Isaac married in 1938 were bleak.

1956

After Ethan and I turned down the football coach, we walked through the woods to the cabin. Even if we'd had the time to play on the football team, it probably would've been one of the worst decisions we ever made.

The starting quarterback and tight end we would've replaced were our classmates. They considered themselves our friends. We knew how important being in the starting lineup on the football team was to both of them. If we took their positions away from them, we probably would've turned them into enemies. Ethan and I had no wish to do that.

They'd seen the coach's interest in us when we played football in gym class, almost always against them.

They spoke with us about it after one of those sessions. We'd spent some time with them in the shower and were toweling ourselves off when the quarterback asked the question.

"Are you guys planning to take our starting positions?"

Ethan laughed. "Don't be silly. Reed and I could never play those positions as well as you do."

"Does the coach see it that way?" the tight end asked.

"Yeah," the quarterback said. "That's the big question."

I knew as well as Ethan did how to lie. "I think the coach is perfectly satisfied with the quarterback and tight end he has now. He told me he plans to win the conference title this year."

"You think," the quarterback asked, "he can do that with us?"

"I don't have any doubt about it," Ethan said. "Reed and I might look good for some plays, but, hell, we're just fooling around in gym class. We've never played in a real game with any pressure on us."

I nodded. "Don't worry about Ethan and me. We're your biggest fans."

The other starting players were also friends of the current starting quarterback and tight end. We couldn't help but wonder if we would've had nothing but enemies for teammates if we'd accepted the coach's offer.

And would they start asking what Ethan and I were doing, in addition to our homework and an occasional game of chess, in our moonshine cabin? They'd undoubtedly heard about it by then.

1956

After we reached the cabin, I kept wondering about Ethan's mother's agreement with his father not to work outside their home.

"Do you think," I asked Ethan, "she's ever regretted her agreement?"

"I'm certain she has," Ethan replied. "She told me she'd hoped to have three or four children. When she could see she'd never have more than one, she asked my father if she might look for a job as a secretary, or for a position in a bank, when I became old enough to fend for myself after school."

"So what did your father have to say about that?"

"He rejected her idea out of hand."

I snickered. "As a total asshole would."

Ethan took a deep breath. "She told me she didn't want to fight with him about it. So that brief discussion, I guess, put an end to it. Anyway, I liked having Mom at home with me."

1956

Despite his increasingly close association with a suspected atheist, Ethan still attended the Meadowlark Church every Sunday morning.

"He always sits with his mother in the first-row-center pew," Marilyn told me. "They both have lovely singing voices."

She'd chosen that Sunday in October, as soon as we'd finished washing and drying the dishes after the noon meal, to accompany me on the path to the cabin and wait for Ethan to arrive.

She loved the gold and yellow oaks and hickories that time of the year as much as I did. The leaves fell gently around us.

My father and I had finished picking and cribbing the corn the previous day. If we hadn't, we'd still be at it even if it was a Sunday. My father would've gladly given up church and one of Reverend Tull's sermons to complete the harvest.

"How do you know," I asked Marilyn, "Ethan and his mother have lovely singing voices? Do you squeeze yourself into that little first-row-center pew with them?"

Marilyn laughed. "No. I still sit in the back of the church with Mom and Dad, where the ambivalent hang out."

"Then how do you know they have lovely singing voices?"

"Hasn't Ethan told you? During some of the songs the congregation sings, all the other people in the church stop singing, sit down and let him and his mother sing alone. Now, whenever that happens, they even turn around and face the congregation. The choir director had suggested they do that. When they do, everybody can hear them better. The people love it. And it's been happening at least once every Sunday."

"I'll be damned. No, Ethan hasn't seen fit to let me know about this."

"After the service is over," Marilyn said, "the people line up to pass by them in the first row, shake their hands and thank them."

Ethan had told me his mother played the piano skilfully and had a beautiful singing voice. Long ago, Ruth's maternal grandmother had given her the upright piano she'd brought to the parsonage when the Tulls moved to Meadowlark. Ruth had taught Ethan how to play the piano and sing long before he began first grade.

Ethan said he couldn't play the piano as well as she did, but she'd insisted he was the better singer. Even during the brief time I'd known him, his voice had deepened.

"One person," Marilyn said, "doesn't care for their singing and popularity at all."

"Who's that?" I asked.

"Ethan's father."

"How do you know what he doesn't care for?"

"He makes it obvious. Whenever they sing by themselves, the look on his face tells everybody how displeased he is."

"Why would he be displeased with their singing Christian hymns in a church?"

Moonshine Cabin

Marilyn shook her head. "He's jealous. He's jealous of his wife and son. Can you believe it? He's supposed to be the one-and-only star of the show at Meadowlark Church. But when they're singing, he's anything but the star."

The next Sunday I went with my family to the church to see and hear for myself the singing duet who'd become the talk of the town. I hadn't told Ethan what I'd learned from Marilyn. Nor had I let him know I'd be at the church.

Marilyn had been adamant we arrive at least 30 minutes before the service was scheduled to begin. Soon after we took our seats, I saw why. The pews were filled. Newcomers had to go down the stairs at the back of the church to the basement and bring up folding chairs to sit on.

"They've come to hear Ethan and his mother sing," Marilyn said. "I told you how popular they are."

"That's why they're here," my mother agreed.

My father nodded. "And Ethan and his mother damned well deserve to be popular."

I watched the people struggling to bring chairs up from the basement.

I rose to my feet. "I can at least help with the chairs."

"No, you can't," Marilyn said.

She pulled on my arm and forced me to sit down again.

She looked at me, shaking her head. "You'll lose your seat."

"I'll lose my seat?" I asked.

"Somebody will take it," my mother said. "And we won't be able to do anything about it. Nobody is allowed to save seats in this church. Ethan's father says Jesus wouldn't allow it."

My father guffawed.

During the service, the first time Ethan and his mother turned around to sing to the congregation, I could tell how surprised they both were to see me.

I had to agree with Marilyn.

43

Ethan and his mother sang beautifully.

I'd known how well Ethan could sing popular music. He'd sung "The Great Pretender," "True Love" and other hit songs for me in the cabin. After the first time I heard him sing, I told him he sang like an angel.

He laughed. "I didn't think you believed in angels."

I also laughed. "That was before I met you."

Now he had his mother's soprano next to his baritone, and they both had the church organ behind them.

In his prepared sermon that Sunday, Reverend Tull argued, at length, drinking alcohol was a sin. Most of his parishioners drank but denied, to him at least, they did. The wine in the wedding-at-Cana story, he said, was actually unfermented grape juice. He was certain a nasty, spirits-loving, Roman Catholic scribe in the Dark Ages had deliberately used the wrong word, wine, and it stuck.

Years ago, the Meadowlark Church board had decided the *blessed are the poor* and *eye of the needle* New Testament passages must've been improperly translated. They voted to forbid their pastors from discussing them. Those remarks were among the best things I'd found when I read the book.

At one point, Reverend Tull chose to depart from his argument. "We must also remember," he said, looking at me, with a sneer, "Jesus never told us the laws carefully set forth in the Old Testament are no longer in effect. He never told us we can somehow go merrily on our way no matter what Leviticus had to say about what we're doing."

I joined the line with my family to thank Ethan and his mother for their singing.

Ethan snickered when I shook his hand. "You finally came to church," he said.

"My family told me about your mother and you singing. I had to hear for myself. You both sound like angels."

Chapter Seven

1956

During the next week, Ethan kept me up-to-date on a battle his mother and father had chosen to fight. The choir director had decided the mimeographed program for the next Sunday should include separate parts for the songs the choir would sing, those the congregation would sing and those Ethan and his mother would sing.

Reverend Tull wouldn't allow it. "The program includes parts for the congregation, the choir and the pastor," he said. "It doesn't include parts for anybody else."

"Not even for your wife and son?" the choir director asked.

Ethan's father shook his head. "They haven't done anything entitling them to a mention on the program."

When Ethan came to see me in the cabin Saturday afternoon, he couldn't wait to tell me what he and his mother had done. "We've become members of the choir."

"You and she should be members of the choir," I said. "You'll add so much to it. They must be very pleased to have you with them."

"Maybe they are, but that's not why we did it."

"Why'd you do it?"

"It gets us around my father's silly rule."

Ethan handed me a copy of the program for the next day's service at the Meadowlark Church.

"As you can see," he said, "there's no mention in this of my mother and me singing. You can see, though, it says 'The Choir Sings' three times and then lists the songs they'll sing. In the old programs the choir always sang twice. The third time in this new program is for when my mother and I sing alone. The program doesn't say that, but everybody will know which songs are the ones we'll sing alone."

"Isn't your father aware of this?"

Ethan laughed. "Not yet. He'll find out tomorrow."

"Why does he have to wait until tomorrow? Doesn't he mimeograph the programs? With that machine you showed me in the basement of the parsonage?"

Ethan laughed. "My father doesn't know how to use that machine. He's never attempted to learn how to use it. He says a minister doesn't mimeograph programs. That's a job for the minister's wife. That's why the machine is in the parsonage basement."

The next day during the noon meal, Marilyn told me Ethan's father had apparently accepted what Ethan and his mother had done— as long as they sat with the choir and the program didn't include their names.

"He still looks awfully unhappy when they sing," Marilyn said. "He's terribly jealous. They get way too much attention. They're attractive too. Ruth might be Ethan's mother, but when they're singing, they look to me like a couple at their wedding, ready to get married and jump into bed together."

Mom and Dad laughed.

I'd noticed how young Ruth appeared to be singing next to her son. Whenever they sang facing one another, they looked as if they might end up kissing.

1956

That was the same day Ethan told me how glad he was we'd boldly ventured across every line in the sand as our intimacy had grown.

"We've found we're free to do," he said, "everything two men who love each other might want to do. Nobody else is ever going to learn what we're doing in this cabin. It's just you and me in here."

Every time we decided to accomplish something new to us, he was the one who'd proposed it. And I never had to think about his proposal more than a moment before I accepted it.

"I'm more than willing," I always said, "to do anything you want us to do."

46

And Ethan always insisted everything we did had to go both ways. Whatever I did for him, he'd do for me, without any exception.

"That's what lovers do," Ethan said.

I don't know how he knew that, but I didn't question it.

So it had gone during the spring and summer of that year.

He'd give me a push, and I'd give in, without hesitation, and let him push me again.

We agreed, at 17, we were totally queer, hopelessly queer. Which meant, of course, we were totally, hopefully queer.

Neither Ethan nor I believed some kind of fate or destiny had brought us together. We both thought our finding one another on the first day of our sophomore year at Meadowlark High was simply our great good luck. And we'd dared to accept it and take it from there.

1956

After supper the next evening, Ethan called to let me know his father had been arrested.

His mother had to withdraw some money from their savings account in the Meadowlark State Bank that afternoon. Then she had to take it to the Kane County courthouse in Geneva.

"Bail money?" I asked.

"Yeah. Otherwise, he'd have to sit on his ass in the jail there until his trial comes up."

"What's he been charged with?"

"My mother doesn't know. All my father will tell her is it's something more serious than a traffic violation. That's why he needed the bail money. He refuses to say anything about it to me. I asked him twice. He said I had no need to know anything about his arrest. He told me not to ask him again."

"Where was your father arrested?" I asked.

"My mother doesn't know that either. It must've been somewhere in Kane County."

"It must've been. But what could a rock-solid minister in a Christian church do that would bring about his arrest?"

"I can't imagine what he did. I've never heard he was involved in anything crooked."

"Except trespassing in my family's woods."

Ethan snickered. "Except that."

1956

The next day, Tuesday, the newscasts and newspapers all included stories about the arrest of Reverend Isaac Tull, the pastor for more than two years at the Meadowlark Church.

The local police had arrested Ethan's father in a truckstop on a busy highway. My family and I knew where the truckstop was. We drove past it whenever we went to the stockyards in Chicago for a sale of our cattle.

The Kane County state's attorney's office had charged Isaac Tull with the *solicitation* of a police officer.

In the cabin the day after that, Ethan brought me up to date on his father's misadventure.

"Now my father tells my mother and other people he was arrested for attempting to bribe a police officer to ignore a traffic violation. He says he's totally innocent. The officer misunderstood what he was attempting to say after the officer told him he was going to ticket him for speeding more than ten miles over the limit."

"Why was your father arrested at a truckstop?"

Ethan shrugged. "My father didn't tell my mother anything about that."

"What was your father doing at the truckstop anyway?"

"He has lunch there sometimes. He tells Mom he likes their cheeseburgers and French fries. He says hers aren't nearly as tasty."

"He got arrested for a speeding violation at a truckstop? Do you believe what he's telling your mother?"

Ethan shrugged again. "I don't know what to think. Neither does my mother. Yeah, somehow, a speeding violation got blown up into an arrest and a criminal charge requiring bail money to keep him out of jail."

I shook my head. "I think way too many things are wrong with your father's story. He's not telling the truth."

1956

Ethan and his mother came to see my family the next Saturday morning.

Marilyn and I got two chairs from the dining room so we could all sit around the kitchen table.

On Wednesday, Ethan's mother told us, his father had gone to see a lawyer in Aurora who handled cases in the criminal court.

"I asked to go with him to see the lawyer," Ruth said. "He wouldn't consider letting me do that. I'm certain he didn't want me to know the actual reasons he was arrested and charged with a crime. He didn't want even his wife to know."

My mother shook her head. "Any husband should want his wife to know precisely why he was arrested, especially if he claims he's innocent."

"I agree with you," Ruth said.

"Can you tell us," my father asked, "if the lawyer will represent Isaac?"

Ruth nodded. "Yes, I can tell you that. He will. I can also tell you the church board has suspended Isaac. He can remain in the parsonage, and they'll continue to pay him a salary, but it will be reduced quite a bit. The board will need to pay for temporary ministers until Isaac's criminal case is resolved."

My mother, who was sitting next to Ruth, took her hand. "Can you and Ethan remain in the parsonage?"

"We can, Annette, but we won't."

49

I turned to Ethan. We sat next to one another at the table. "Where will you live?" I asked.

"Let me explain," Ruth said. "Yesterday, I also went to Aurora to see a lawyer. I hired him to represent me. I'm leaving Isaac. My lawyer will file my divorce papers on Monday. I'm asking for custody of Ethan. My lawyer says he's certain any judge assigned to my case will grant me custody of Ethan."

Ethan turned to me. "The judge will ask me if I want to live with my mother or father. I'll tell the judge I definitely want to live with my mother. I can't imagine living alone with my father. Mom's lawyer says the judge will grant me my wish because I'm 17."

Ethan had previously told me living alone with his father would be hell. He'd have to run away and hope I'd run with him.

Ruth sighed. "And that brings us to our problem."

Ethan nodded. "Yes, it does."

Ruth continued. "I'll live with my mother in Aurora. You know, that's the house I grew up in. Ever since my father died five years ago, she's lived by herself in that house. She says she's terribly lonely. She'd very much like to have another person living with her. And she tells me she'll be very glad if I'm that person."

Ethan had told me his grandmother's house was on the east side of the Fox River. His maternal grandfather had worked in an east-side factory making construction machinery.

"But you see," Ruth said, "I want Ethan to finish high school here in Meadowlark. So does he."

She had tears in her eyes.

My mother squeezed her hand.

"Of course he should," my father said. "And there's an easy way to solve the problem. Ethan can live here with us. Reed's bed is big enough for both of them to sleep on."

Ethan reached for my hand under the table and squeezed it.

I squeezed back.

Chapter Eight

1956

Marilyn got up from her chair, found the box of tissues we kept in a kitchen cabinet, brought it to the table and handed it to Ruth.

"Yes," I said, "my bed is more than big enough for both Ethan and me."

My family's house had three bedrooms, all of them on the second floor. My mother and father occupied the most spacious one, but Marilyn's bedroom and mine were both big enough for two people.

My father turned to me. "You must have room in your closet for Ethan's clothes."

"I sure do," I replied. "I can give him half the drawers in my dresser too. We can easily fit ourselves and our stuff into my room."

I hadn't imagined Reverend Tull's strange arrest would bring Ethan and me such bliss—sleeping together every night in the same bed.

Ethan turned to my father. "If I'm going to live here, I want to do as much work as Reed does on your farm. I want to earn my keep."

My father chuckled. "We can let you do that."

That morning Ethan and his mother had taken most of her clothes and personal items to her mother's house in Aurora. Ethan had driven his grandmother's ten-year-old Chevrolet back to Meadowlark. Ethan's mother would use that car from then on.

After Ruth and Ethan's discussion with my family around our kitchen table, they drove to Meadowlark to remove his clothes and personal items from the parsonage and bring them back to our house.

The bliss began that very night for Ethan and me.

1956

The next morning Ethan and I went with my family to the church for the Sunday services. Ethan and his mother, who'd driven out from

Aurora with her mother, sang together in the choir as they'd done before. They intended to continue doing that in the future.

Ethan's father sat in the front-row-center pew, alone.

1956

When Ethan and I walked to the cabin after school let out the next Tuesday, I asked him about his mother's divorce case.

"My father has already agreed to it," he said. "He had no objection to her having custody of me. She told me the final divorce decree will specifically allow her to have me live with your family while I'm still going to school in Meadowlark."

"Your father isn't contesting any of that?"

"He isn't contesting a damned thing."

"Even if your mother has custody of you, won't you still have to spend some time with him?"

"My mom's lawyer says the word for that is *visitation*."

"Whatever they call it, won't you have to spend some time with your father?"

Ethan laughed. "No, I won't. I told my mom I don't want to spend any of my time with that man. She told her lawyer what I said. He spoke with my father's lawyer. You know what?"

"What?"

"My father agreed. He doesn't want to spend time with me anymore than I want to spend time with him."

"He's a father who doesn't want to spend time with his son?"

Ethan laughed again. "I'm getting a divorce from that asshole just as much as my mom is."

We reached the cabin and started a fire.

Knowing I was curious, Ethan told me more about his mother and father.

They'd met when they attended Wheaton College in the 1930s. Ruth had gone to college to obtain the education she'd convinced her mother and father she needed in the 20th Century. Some scholarship money had helped her do it. Isaac had gone to Wheaton College to become a Christian minister like his father before him.

They married the day after they graduated in 1938.

The board of a church in a small town in southern Indiana had agreed to hire Isaac Tull as its minister. It could only offer him a minimal salary and its parsonage for his home, but he thought it would be a good start for him in his career as a minister.

The board set one condition on Isaac Tull's employment. He had to be married. If he was to be their preacher, he had to have a wife living with him in the parsonage.

Isaac asked Ethan's mother to help him meet that condition.

She'd diligently searched for but hadn't found a single opportunity for employment, not even as a secretary or a clerk.

She admitted to Ethan she'd found Isaac physically attractive then. He'd played on the football team all four of his years in college, but always as a substitute, never as a starter.

He was also, she'd told Ethan, the most gentlemanly man she'd dated in college. The others had all wanted to have sex with her. Without the benefit of a marriage, though, she'd never agree to that.

She knew Isaac Tull wouldn't be the husband of her dreams, but she could imagine living a pleasant married life with him.

She told Ethan her and his father's sex life began the night of their marriage and ended a month later, as soon as she realized she was pregnant with Ethan. After that, she and Isaac never slept together again, not even in the same room.

During her pregnancy, Isaac used that as his excuse not to have intercourse with her. After she gave birth to Ethan, she assumed Isaac no longer found her sexually attractive.

"But she chose," I asked, "to remain in a loveless marriage?"

Ethan chuckled. "It was a loveless marriage for him, but it was a marriage filled with love for her and me. She taught me how to read long before I started going to school. She taught me math, science, geography, history and so much more. She kindled my interest in current events. We read the newspapers and all sorts of magazines and books together. And on top of it all, she taught me how to sing and play the piano."

"Did your father encourage her to do that with you?"

Ethan scoffed. "He didn't have anything good to say about whatever we did together. I assumed he believed we were wasting our time. He said we should've been reading the bible, memorizing it word for word. Other than that, he never seemed to care much what I did—not until you came along. Then he cared intensely. He told me I didn't need you for a friend. Then he wouldn't let you set foot inside our house. Then he came here and told your family you and I were going to hell. It was as if my friendship with you drove him nuts. I never understood any of that. He always said we were supposed to attempt to convert atheists, not turn our backs on them."

"You've never attempted to convert me."

"You don't need to convert. Nobody will keep you out of any heaven I'm in. It wouldn't be Christian."

Like Ethan, his mother and father were their parents' only children. Ethan was five when his paternal grandfather died and ten when his paternal grandmother died. He had no aunts, uncles or first cousins. He knew he had more distant cousins, but he'd never met them. He was left with a mother, a father and a maternal grandmother.

Regarding the quantity of relatives in our lives, I couldn't claim I was much better off than Ethan. I only had a mother, a father, a sister and the great-aunt who lived with our landlady.

1956

After Ethan moved into my family's house, he and I slept, ate, worked, studied and did everything else we did together.

We took the bus to school with Marilyn. She and we washed and dried the dishes after every meal we consumed at home.

Moonshine Cabin

Ethan helped me carry the pails of ground corn and cobs to the feeding troughs for the cattle twice a day. I showed him how to break bales of hay in the hayloft on the second-story of the barn and pitchfork it through the holes in the floor above the hay feeders below.

He helped me shovel the manure off the barn floor and spread bales of new straw in its place. I showed him how to operate the tractor when we pulled the manure spreader from the manure piles behind the barn out to the harvested corn fields.

"The manure is our fertilizer for next year's crops," I explained.

I showed him what we had to do to keep the chickens fed, their eggs taken from their nests, and their manure removed from the henhouse and their outdoor area next to it. I planned to show him what we'd need to do in the spring to plant and weed the vegetable garden. We always saved the chicken manure for the garden.

Ethan laughed. "You're making me a farm boy, just like you."

I planned to go with Ethan and my family to the Meadowlark Church every Sunday. I wanted to hear him sing with his mother. And unlike his father, the temporary ministers didn't give me the evil eye during their sermons.

Within days after Ruth Tull moved into her mother's house, she obtained a position in the accounting department of one of the largest banks in Aurora. She'd majored in mathematics in college and had taken courses in accounting.

She told Ethan she was going to begin saving her earnings to help put him through college. Although her mother lived on the paltry pension and Social Security benefits Ethan's grandfather had earned, she had no mortgage on her house. She refused to consider taking rent money from her daughter to live with her.

Ruth used her first earnings from the bank to pay professional movers to retrieve her piano from the parsonage and take it back to the house it was in when she'd taught herself how to play it.

Her lawyer told her now that she earned far more than Isaac did, the judge would let her waive alimony and child support.

1956

The people in Meadowlark who dared to speak with Reverend Isaac Tull reported he claimed he was a totally innocent person who'd been wrongly accused of committing a crime. He could only imagine the officer who'd arrested him had strangely misunderstood something he'd said.

When the people who spoke with him asked him specifically what crime he'd been charged with, he said it was what the newspapers had said it was, *solicitation*. When they asked him why that was a crime, he said he didn't know. Not even his lawyer could explain it for him.

The people who spoke with him also said he appeared to be in a deep depression. They wondered if losing his wife and son had caused it.

Ethan laughed when I told him that.

"You and I both know," he said, "my father is damned pleased my mother and I have left the parsonage. I can't remember a time in my life when he didn't act as if he put up with her and me living in the same house with him only because he had to—only because he was her husband and my father."

"That's sad. You can be glad you have a very loving mother."

"My father wasn't the least bit loving. It took him no time at all to agree to divorce my mother and give up custody of me. And he knew I'd be sleeping in the same bed with you."

"He knew that?"

"My mother made sure he knew where and with whom I'd be sleeping. She saw no reason to keep it a secret from him. She actually made me think she very much wanted him to know it. Yeah, he's well aware I'm sleeping every night now in the same bed with that damned good-looking atheist farmer boy he can't tolerate."

"That *snotty* atheist farmer boy," I said.

Ethan laughed. "Yeah, *that* one."

56

Chapter Nine

1956

Reverend Tull still saw his son and wife—his soon-to-be ex-wife—in church every Sunday morning. They said he never made any attempt to speak with them.

Nor did they make any attempt to speak with him.

Whenever I thought about Ethan's family, I felt awfully glad I lived with my mother, father and sister on a cattle farm with a woods in the heart of the American Midwest—and now, wonder of wonders, with Ethan as well.

1956

On the other hand, we weren't allowed to pass through that autumn without a reminder we lived in a larger world that sometimes outrageously threatened to kill us all. Ethan and I followed the Suez Crisis daily. This time, Marilyn joined us.

After President Nasser of Egypt nationalized the Suez Canal, the armed forces of Britain, France and Israel seized the canal. The leader of the Soviet Union, Nikita Khrushchev, threatened to begin nothing less than a nuclear war if the aggressors didn't undo what they'd done. President Eisenhower of the United States, on the eve of his reelection, asked the country's three allies to give up the canal.

We all breathed sighs of relief when they did. We weren't prepared for a nuclear war over the ownership of the Suez Canal.

Most of the people living in or near Meadowlark didn't like Ike. They'd voted for Senator Robert Taft of Ohio in the presidential primary in 1952. I remembered them wailing when their guy lost the nomination at the Republican convention in Chicago that summer.

They said Eisenhower should've run as a Democrat.

"That's what he is," they said, as if that were as blameworthy as being an atheist or a queer.

Ron Fritsch

1956

When my mother and father sent their annual holiday messages to Marilyn's and my grandparents that year, the family photographs included Ethan. My parents said Ethan was my best friend and was now living with us. They made no attempt to explain why.

1957

We had to wait until the latter half of April for the trial of Ethan's father. Since neither my father, mother or sister needed to use our car that Monday, Ethan and I drove to Aurora early in the morning, picked up his mother and drove on to the courthouse in Geneva. We'd obtained excused absences from school for the day.

During the drive, Ruth told Ethan and me her divorce lawyer had kept her up to date on Isaac's case. That was how she knew the judge had scheduled the case for trial that day.

Her lawyer had also told her what would happen. Isaac had agreed to waive a jury trial. He had two reasons to do so.

His attorney had no doubt informed him a jury would be more likely to convict him than a judge would. And if Isaac insisted upon a trial before a jury, it would consume many days on the judge's calendar. If the jury found Isaac guilty, the judge he'd angered by asking for a jury trial would give him the maximum penalty.

Ruth's lawyer had learned from a friend in the state's attorney's office Isaac Tull had declined an offer from the assistant state's attorney handling his case. If Isaac pleaded guilty, the prosecution would ask the judge to sentence him to probation. Isaac would serve no time in prison.

"I assume," Ruth said, "Isaac feared he'd lose his job anyway."

1957

We entered the courtroom and sat down in the gallery.

A bailiff soon approached us. "I'm sorry," he said to Ethan's mother, "the judge will only let adults attend this trial."

He looked at Ethan and me.

"These boys," he said, "will have to leave."

"Just a moment," Ruth said. "These two young men are no longer children. They're both eighteen." She touched Ethan's shoulder. "Ethan Tull here is the defendant's son, his only child. I'm Ethan's mother. Ethan is the only relative the defendant has left."

She nodded toward me, sitting along the aisle on the other side of Ethan.

"Reed," she said, "is Ethan's best friend. I believe they're both mature enough to hear anything anybody will say in this trial."

"How old are you?" the bailiff asked me.

"Eighteen," I said, showing him my driver's license.

He asked Ethan the same question and received the same reply. Ethan also showed him his driver's license.

The bailif took a deep breath. "I'll speak to the judge."

He exited the courtroom through the doorway behind the judge's bench. He returned ten minutes later and approached us again.

He spoke, looking at Ethan's mother. "The judge said your son and his friend may attend the trial."

Ruth nodded her head. "Please thank the judge for us."

"Why does our age matter?" I asked her.

"I haven't the faintest idea," she replied.

1957

Ethan's father entered the courtroom with an older gray-haired man. They both wore black suits as if they were attending a funeral.

"He must be with his lawyer," Ruth said.

When they walked down the aisle on their way to the table the defendants and their attorneys sat at, Ethan's father stared straight ahead as he passed us.

Ethan looked at me and snickered. "He wasn't at all pleased to see *us* here."

Two older men from Meadowlark entered the courtroom. They nodded when they saw us. They both owned farms in the township.

"They're on the church board," Ethan's mother said.

"They'll report back to the full board?" Ethan asked.

Ruth nodded. "That must be why they're here."

A group of people nodded toward Ethan's mother when they saw her. They walked past us and took seats in the first row of the gallery. The bailiffs had let only two other people sit in that row.

"They're reporters," Ethan's mother told us. "They came to the parsonage the day Isaac was arrested. They identified themselves and the television stations and newspapers they worked for. They wanted my comment on the arrest. I declined. I saw no reason to speak with them. Besides, I had to hurry to the bank to withdraw the bail money before it closed for the day. My mother was on her way from Aurora to drive me here."

"Were the reporters all in a group that day?" I asked.

Ruth nodded. "Yes, they were. They arrived at the parsonage about the same time and rang the front-door bell. I made them wait on the front porch until I was ready to walk to the bank and get the bail money. To be polite, I stopped long enough to find out who they were and let them know I had nothing to say to them. They followed me to the bank. They waited outside until my mother came by to pick me up and bring me here."

"Vultures," Ethan said.

His mother chuckled. "They were doing their jobs then. They're doing their jobs now. The defendant was the pastor of the Meadowlark Church. A person in a position like that isn't supposed to be arrested and tried for committing a serious crime."

"They had a scandal thrust upon them," I said. "What could they do but go where it took them?"

Ruth looked at me and smiled. "Precisely," she said.

Moonshine Cabin

1957

The judge hearing what the clerk would call *the People versus Isaac Tull* entered the courtroom from the door behind his bench. He was heavyset, had a full head of gray hair and wore thick glasses.

He turned to the assistant state's attorney, who sat alone at the table for the prosecutors. "You may call your first witness."

As the person called got up from his seat in the front row of the gallery and walked to the witness stand, Ethan and I simultaneously nudged each other.

The prosecution's first witness was a man who appeared to be in his early 20s. He had brown crewcut hair and broad shoulders. He undoubtedly worked out. He had the body of a well-trained defensive back in football.

When he sat down at the witness stand, we could see he was cleanly shaven and had eyes the color of the sky on a cloudless day. I was certain Marilyn would tell us this man's good looks in a Hollywood movie would make a lot of hearts throb, including her own.

He testified he was a police officer. On the day he arrested the defendant he was on duty in plainclothes in the truckstop located in the town that employed him.

When the witness first saw the defendant that day in the truckstop, he appeared to be loitering near the entrance to the men's room. The witness entered it, went to the single row of urinals, unzipped the fly of his jeans and prepared to urinate.

"Where in hell is this taking us?" Ethan whispered.

"We can leave," his mother whispered back.

Ethan shook his head and whispered again. "I'm not leaving. I want to see where this goes."

Isaac's attorney objected to the word *loitering*. "Does the witness claim he could read the defendant's mind?"

The judge denied the objection and let the word stand. "The witness said the defendant appeared to him to be loitering."

The witness next testified that, soon after he began urinating, the defendant walked to the urinal nearest him on his left. The witness and the defendant were the only persons in the men's room at that time. The defendant could've chosen another urinal.

"The defendant stared at my penis," the witness said. "Then he asked me if I'd let him perform an act of oral sex on me."

The spectators in the gallery, including Ruth and I, gasped.

"Jesus Christ," Ethan whispered.

The witness wasn't done. "The defendant didn't actually use the words *oral sex*."

The judge glanced at Ethan and me and turned to the witness. "You won't need to tell us the words the defendant actually used."

The two farmers from Meadowlark looked at one another and shook their heads as if the witness had proclaimed the end of the world.

I understood why the judge wouldn't let us know which words Reverend Tull had allegedly used for *oral sex*. I was still disappointed we wouldn't hear them.

"How," the assistant state's attorney asked the witness, "did you respond to the defendant's offer to perform an act of oral sex on you?"

"I asked the defendant where he'd do that."

"What did the defendant say in response to your question?"

"He said he could do it in one of the toilet stalls. He'd lock the door behind us. He told me nobody who came into the men's room would be able to tell two people were in the stall with the door closed. They'd assume one person was urinating or defecating in the stall."

"What did you do then?" the assistant state's attorney asked.

The witness stared at Reverend Isaac Tull, seated next to his attorney at the table for the defendants. "I showed the defendant my police badge. I informed him I was arresting him for solicitation. I handcuffed him and took him to the unmarked car I drove that day."

The assistant state's attorney turned to the judge. "I have no more questions for this witness."

Chapter Ten

1957

The judge turned to Isaac's attorney. "Cross-examination, counsel?" Isaac's attorney rose from his chair at the defendants' table and walked to the witness stand.

He looked down at his notes before he began his first question. "When you spoke with the defendant Reverend Tull at the urinals in the men's room, you had an erection, didn't you?"

The crowd in the courtroom murmured.

The witness scoffed. "Of course not. I'd never allow that to happen in a public place."

"And *you* asked Reverend Tull to perform oral sex on you."

The witness shook his head. "I'd never ask another man to perform oral sex on me. The thought of it fills me with disgust."

"Are you aware committing perjury in this court could lead you to prison?"

"As a police officer, I'm well aware of that. But I haven't committed perjury in this court or any other court."

Isaac's attorney had no more questions for the witness.

The next witness the assistant state's attorney called was, like his first witness, an attractive man who appeared to be in his 20s. He testified he was a police officer for one of the larger towns in Kane County. At all times relevant to his testimony, he said, he was working in plainclothes with the police in the town in which the defendant was arrested.

He testified he hadn't been in the courtroom when the first witness for the prosecution testified, and he hadn't heard any of his testimony.

He'd also seen the defendant loitering outside the men's room in the truckstop. That sighting was five days before the defendant's arrest. Then too, the defendant followed him into the men's room and stood next to him at the urinals.

The witness and the defendant were the only persons in the men's room at the time. The defendant could've chosen another urinal.

The defendant stared at the witness's penis and offered to perform an act of oral sex on him. The defendant told the witness he could do it in a stall locked from the inside, and nobody coming into the men's room would discover what they were doing.

The officer testified he bluntly told the defendant he didn't want a homosexual going down on him and asked him to go away and leave him alone. The defendant did so.

Isaac's attorney began his cross-examination of the officer with two statements. "You didn't arrest the defendant. You didn't believe he committed a crime in his conversation with you."

"He committed a crime," the officer said. "It's called solicitation. He offered to perform a criminal act with me. But the local police were building a case against him that would stand up in court. Usually, defendants in these cases will try to argue a police officer somehow enticed them into offering to perform a sexual act with them they otherwise never would've considered doing. They call that entrapment. But when a defendant does it with more than one officer, as this defendant did, he's demonstrated nobody had to lure him into breaking the law."

The third prosecution witness was a police officer employed by another of the larger towns in Kane County. He also appeared to be in his 20s and was as fit and attractive as the first two witnesses.

He also said he hadn't been in the courtroom when the two preceding witnesses testified. He hadn't heard any of their testimony.

At all times relevant to his testimony, he was, like the second witness, working in plainclothes with the police in the town in which the defendant was arrested.

The third officer had also seen the defendant loitering outside the men's room in the truck stop. That was two days before the defendant's arrest. And, once again, the defendant followed the witness into the men's room and, despite having his pick of every urinal in the place, chose one next to the one the witness had selected.

After the defendant offered to perform an act of oral sex on him, the witness told the defendant he'd rather die than spend a moment of his life in a toilet stall with a homosexual.

The fourth witness rose from his seat in the first row. He wore bib overalls and appeared to be in his 50s. He'd used a bank loan and his savings as a construction worker to buy the truckstop a year ago.

He'd observed the defendant "and others of his ilk" offering to perform various sexual services for his youthful male customers. Some of those customers were truck drivers who'd gone a number of days, maybe even a week or more, since the last time they'd had sex with their wives or girlfriends.

"I couldn't blame *them*," the truckstop owner testified, glaring at Ethan's father, "but I didn't want that homosexual stuff going on in my place of business. The previous owner might've considered it an amenity for some of his customers, but I didn't share that way of thinking. I'd bought a place for people to buy gas and eat a nice meal, not a place to have illicit sex in a toilet."

"Did you take any action," the assistant state's attorney asked, "to rid yourself of the problem?"

"I sure did."

"What did you do?"

"I asked each of those perverts to leave my truckstop and never come back. Most of them, I'm happy to say, complied with my request. But the defendant was defiant. I started calling the cops every time I saw him come into the truckstop. The cops agreed to send plainclothes officers whenever they were available. The third time the officers caught him soliciting them for sex they arrested him. Needless to say, he hasn't come back to the truckstop since the day of his arrest. You can't believe how pleased I am with what those officers did."

Isaac's attorney chose not to cross-examine the third and fourth witnesses for the prosecution.

After they testified, all four of the prosecution witnesses took seats in the front row of the gallery. The reporters opened up enough space for them to sit together, shoulder to shoulder, comrades in the ancient but endless struggle against the horror of homosexuality.

1957

Reverend Tull's attorney called his client to the witness stand to testify in his defense. Isaac well remembered meeting the police officer who arrested him in the truckstop. He'd gone there for lunch that day. After his arrival, he'd decided it would be best if he paid a visit to the men's room before he sat down at the counter and ordered his food.

Isaac's attorney nodded. "Do you agree with the police officer's description of your meeting with him?"

Reverend Tull shook his head. "I don't agree with any of it. Nothing happened the way the police officer testified it did."

"Please tell the court what actually happened, what you said, and what the officer said."

"First of all, I didn't approach him. I was already urinating when he approached me. He ended up at the urinal on my right. He could've chosen any of the other urinals. He was correct in saying nobody else was in the men's room when he and I were."

"What happened then?"

"I could see, out of the corner of my eye, after he unzipped the fly of his jeans, he began stroking his penis. He kept stroking it to the point where he appeared to be fully erect. I was astonished a person would do that sort of thing in a public place in front of a perfect stranger. I've led a life in which such things simply don't happen."

During his testimony, Ethan's father glared at the police officer who'd arrested him.

That officer, though, was looking at the judge and shaking his head.

"What happened then?" Isaac's attorney asked.

"The officer asked me if I wanted to perform an act of oral sex on him. Although those weren't the words he actually used that day."

The judge thought it best to intervene again. "You don't need to tell this court the words he actually used. You may continue with your testimony."

"The officer told me I could do it in one of the toilet stalls. We'd lock the door behind us. Anybody who came into the men's room would assume only one person was in the stall, not two guys having sex."

"What happened then?"

"I told him he belonged in a mental institution. I couldn't imagine why he'd believe I'd have any interest in having any kind of sex with another man. I informed him I've been a Christian my entire life. I finished urinating, zipped up my pants and prepared to leave. Then he showed me his police badge and told me I was under arrest. I didn't believe the police could so dishonestly arrest a person in America."

Ethan's father also remembered seeing the two other police officers who'd testified. Just as the arresting officer had done, both of them had gotten erections at a urinal next to his. Both of them had asked him to perform an act of oral sex on them.

"They both lied," Reverend Tull said, "when they told this court I offered to perform an act of oral sex on them. I can't imagine doing such a thing. I'm a devout Christian."

Reverend Tull testified the owner of the truckstop had never asked him to leave the place.

"I've never spoken with that man," Isaac said. "I saw him sometimes when I went there for lunch. I never knew he was the owner of the truckstop. I thought maybe he pumped gas."

When Reverend Tull stepped down from the witness stand and walked to the defendants' table, he was in tears.

1957

"Your Honor," the assistant state's attorney said during his closing argument, "the four prosecution witnesses had nothing to gain from coming into this court and telling your honor anything other than the sordid truth concerning the defendant and his criminal activities in the men's room at the truckstop in question. No, it's crystal clear to any reasonable person the prosecution witnesses told the truth, and the defendant did nothing in this court today but lie. The four prosecution witnesses were out to rid the truckstop of a male homosexual offering to perform criminal sexual services for male customers in the men's room. We can all be very pleased the officers who testified succeeded in stopping him."

The judge stared at Ethan's father.

The assistant state's attorney continued. "Now the time has come, Your Honor, to render a guilty verdict and sentence the defendant to a term in prison that will let him and other homosexuals know there's no place for them and their wicked activities in a civilized world."

Isaac's attorney could only argue, in his closing remarks for his client, the four prosecution witnesses had brazenly lied.

After the closing arguments, the judge rendered his verdict as Ethan's father and his lawyer stood before him like schoolchildren whose teacher had sent to face a stern and unforgiving principal.

"Reverend Tull," the judge said, "I fully believe the witnesses for the prosecution told the truth in this court. I'm convinced, well beyond a reasonable doubt, you offered to perform a criminal act with the three officers who testified. You'd no doubt offered to perform the same despicable act with other men you'd accosted in that men's room. You had to be stopped from what you were doing. Your arrest did that. I therefore find you guilty as charged."

The assistant state's attorney rose to his feet. "Can we proceed, Your Honor, to sentencing?"

The judge turned to Ethan's father. "This court sentences you to one year in a state prison. That should send a message to you—and to others of your kind—a man soliciting another man for sex in a men's room is a horrific crime. A person who does it deserves substantial time in prison. That has to be at least a year."

Chapter Eleven

1957

Reverend Tull spoke to his attorney in a whisper even the judge probably couldn't hear. The two older farmers from Meadowlark looked at one another and shook their heads again.

"Your Honor," Isaac's attorney said, "Reverend Tull asks you to please give him sufficient time to put his affairs in order."

The judge nodded. "I'll give your client seven days to put his affairs in order. No later than nine a.m. one week from today, he'll report to the Kane County sheriff's office. They'll transport him to the prison. I'm certain you'll advise him he may file an appeal and ask the appellate court to stay his sentence pending his appeal. The judges in that court will decide if any further delay is warranted in this case."

1957

For our trip from Geneva to Aurora, Ethan and his mother accepted my offer to drive while they both sat on the back seat.

Ethan broke our silence. "I can't imagine how that liar thinks he'll ever get into heaven."

"You think," I asked, "those police officers and the owner of the truckstop told the truth?"

"Like the judge," Ethan replied, "I have no doubt they did. Dad admitted he was in that john three times in five days discussing oral sex with three damned good-looking police officers. He was hanging out there. If, as he said, those officers came up to him and showed him their private parts, why didn't he run away immediately? Why would a devout Christian wait even a moment to hear their requests for oral sex?"

"That's a good point," Ruth said. "I thought about that too."

I glanced at Ruth in the rearview mirror. "Did you ever suspect he was homosexual?"

"I'd wondered if he was," Ruth replied. "His wanting to have sex with men would explain why he didn't want to have sex with me, the woman he married, the woman he set up to seem to be his wife."

"And there he was," Ethan said, "offering to perform oral sex on strangers in a toilet stall."

"I hadn't imagined," Ruth said, "he'd stoop that low."

I had another question. "I wonder how he found out what was going on in the men's room at that truckstop."

In the rearview mirror, I could see Ruth shrugging. "Since we moved to Meadowlark, he's been going to a lot of meetings, at least once every two weeks, of a bible-study group. They meet all over northern Illinois. He says they and he are like-minded in their views on scripture. He became very friendly with one of the participants, a man. Whenever Isaac spoke with him on the telephone, he made me leave the kitchen. I needed to do that, he told me, in order for him and his friend to have a private conversation. Whenever Ethan came near the kitchen, Isaac immediately terminated the call. I wonder if maybe he and his friend are like-minded in more ways than one."

Ethan had told me about the bible-study group, but not about the friend or the telephone calls. Ethan said his father had never hosted a meeting of the group at the parsonage in Meadowlark.

"Do you think," I asked, "he'll file an appeal to stay out of prison for a while longer?"

"I doubt it," Ruth replied. "He doesn't have any more money to pay his lawyer. He's used up what little savings he had. If the church board fires him, he won't have any income. He won't have a place to live. He'll be better off in prison. At least there he'll have food to eat and a roof over his head."

"Maybe," Ethan said, "the church board will give him some severance pay."

His mother scoffed. "Those self-righteous, wealthy farmers in Meadowlark? They won't give him, a convicted homosexual with a year to serve in prison, a dime of their hard-earned money."

1957

We were in Aurora. "Did you know," Ethan asked his mother, "what he was accusing Reed and me of doing in our cabin in the woods?"

Ruth sighed. "I knew."

"Did you care," Ethan asked, "whether he was right or not?"

We reached the street Ruth lived on with her mother.

"No," she replied. "I believe what you and Reed do in your cabin is something for you and him to decide upon. I'm quite certain you wouldn't be the first two men who loved one another as intensely as your father believes you do."

I stopped the car outside her mother's house.

"Otherwise," she asked, "why would the Old Testament bother to prohibit it? The Greeks and Romans seemed to think it was perfectly okay. Both Alexander the Great and Frederick the Great did too."

1957

During the drive from Aurora to Meadowlark, Ethan sat on the front seat with me.

"I think it's obvious," I said, "those police officers weren't randomly chosen to nail your father."

Ethan laughed. "Whoever selected them must've gone through all the police departments in the county to come up with those guys. I think part of my father's testimony was honest. They must've had erections—to make him think they wanted him to go down on them."

"They would've wanted to tease him into making an offer."

72

"They would've wanted him to see what they had. And I bet those guys damned well enjoyed flaunting what they have—especially to a desperate queer who could want it but never touch it."

"I don't doubt you're right."

"But they could never admit any of that in court."

I nodded. "Like you and the judge, I'm certain your father did what those officers said he did. But I don't think what he did should be a crime. What he was proposing to do with those officers is something we do now whenever we please. We don't think of it as a crime."

Ethan snickered. "Hell, no, we don't."

"I hope," I said, "I'm never reduced to asking a stranger for sex in a john. But your father did say they'd lock the door behind them. If they were careful, nobody coming into the men's room would know two guys were in a stall having sex."

"But the owner of the truckstop didn't want that sort of thing going on in his men's room. What about him? Shouldn't he have a right to operate his business as he wishes?"

"He could've had your father arrested for trespass, when he showed up in the place after he was asked to leave and never come back. I doubt a judge would give anybody a year in prison for doing that. Maybe a few days in a jail or a fine. But I certainly don't believe a man having sex with another man in a private place should be sent to prison for a goddamned year."

"I agree," Ethan said. "That shouldn't be a crime. When I'm having sex with you, I don't feel as if we're doing anything wrong. I feel as if we've somehow gotten ourselves into a heaven all our own."

I laughed. "That's how I feel too."

1957

Ethan and I arrived home in time to do our usual chores and eat supper with my family around the kitchen table. We told them what had happened in court that day.

"My father admitted," Ethan said, "three times in five days he had conversations in the men's room at the truckstop with police officers in plainclothes, and they were talking about him performing oral sex on them. No traffic violation was involved."

My father shook his head. "That man is a fraud."

My mother turned to Ethan. "And after what your father accused you and Reed of doing. He was doing that with perfect strangers in a men's room. Then he lied and told everybody he was arrested for a traffic violation that somehow escalated into something else."

Marilyn snickered. "And he was a minister in a church."

I snickered too. "He was the second minister in a row at the Meadowlark Church who was guilty of hypocrisy in the first degree. And both cases involved illicit sex."

1957

The next day at school nobody said a word to either Ethan or me about his father's conviction and prison sentence. The story had been in the evening newscasts the day before and the newspapers that morning.

During lunch Marilyn came to Ethan and me and explained it.

"They're being polite," she said to Ethan. "They've assumed you don't want to talk about it."

"I'm grateful to them," Ethan said.

I shrugged. "What's to say anyway about a queer-hating minister offering to provide oral sex to strangers in a truckstop men's room?"

Marilyn laughed. "I can't think of one goddamned thing to say."

1957

When Ethan and I walked to our cabin after school, the springtime woods seemed unchanged from our first walk in them together two years earlier. But our lives had gone through nothing but change.

Moonshine Cabin

When we came upon the cattle grazing again in the sunlit glade, Ethan took my arm and made me stop.

"My father," he said, "knew we were queer even before we did. He knew it from the start, the day he found out we were friends."

"Yeah, he knew because he was queer himself. But I don't understand why he gave us so much trouble."

Ethan snickered. "He gave us trouble because he hated what we had going. He could see we were in love when we were doing our homework in my room in the parsonage. And we were, too."

Ethan was right about that. We were doing our homework in his room in the parsonage because we'd fallen in love.

"And that's why," Ethan said, "he barred you from the parsonage. He didn't want to see what he saw when you were there. I had a nice, bright, great-looking guy for my boyfriend, and he'd never had anybody close to that. He didn't want me to have what he could never ever allow himself to have."

"You think that was his problem?"

"I'm as sure about it as I am the sun will rise in the east tomorrow morning. He could've tried to find himself a boyfriend when he was younger. My mother showed me pictures of him in his football uniform in college. But no, he thought the Old Testament wouldn't let him have a boyfriend. He'd go to hell if he did."

I suspected Ethan was right.

"My mother wondered if my father was queer. Since he didn't have a boyfriend when he was young and needed one, like you and me, he was offering free oral sex in the men's room at a truckstop. He was that desperate for any kind of physical connection to another man."

"I feel sorry for him," I said. "A life as a queer minister can't be much fun."

"He chose that life. Maybe he didn't choose to be queer, but he did choose to be a minister. But you go ahead and feel sorry for him if you wish. Maybe I should too. He's been totally fucked up every day of all the days I can remember knowing him."

"You were three or four years old, and you already knew he was fucked up?"

"I did. Let's face it. He was deeply jealous. The first time he saw you, he knew damned well what we were gonna do, sooner or later. He couldn't stand it. It drove him nuts."

Chapter Twelve

1957

The next day, Wednesday, the two elderly members of the Meadowlark Church board who'd attended the trial paid a visit to the parsonage with the board's attorney.

They told Ethan's father the board had voted unanimously to fire him, effective immediately. Because he'd already received his salary for the month, the church owed him nothing more.

The attorney gave Reverend Tull a notice demanding he vacate the parsonage. The attorney told him if he remained in the parsonage beyond the days allowed him in the notice, the board would file an eviction suit. If he didn't obey the judge's eviction order, the sheriff would put him and his possessions on the street.

Ruth was right. If Ethan's father didn't go to prison, he wouldn't have shelter or money to stay alive. In prison he'd at least have a roof over his head and food, such as it might be, to eat.

1957

After lunch and the dishes on Saturday, Ethan and I walked to the cabin. A morning rainstorm had left the fields too wet for the spring work in them we and my father had hoped to accomplish that day.

When we reached the top of the valley on the north side of the creek, we could see something dark hanging down from the tree nearest the cabin, which was one of the largest oaks in the woods.

I wondered if a high limb had broken off in the wind in the storm and gotten caught in the lower branches when it fell.

But as we neared the cabin, what we could see hanging from the lowest limb of the tree became a man in his Sunday suit as black and bleak as hell itself. He had a rope tied in a noose around his neck.

Behind the hanging man, on the path from Meadowlark, we saw Reverend Isaac Tull's 1938 Chevrolet.

When we reached Ethan's father, we could see he'd stood on a three-foot stepladder he kicked over when he was ready to die.

He must've done it early that morning, before the storm. His clothes were still soaked.

I pointed toward the stepladder. "Is that from the parsonage?"

Ethan nodded. "Yeah. So is the rope. I've seen them in the basement. They were there when we moved into the parsonage."

We were careful not to touch anything. We didn't want to leave fingerprints. We didn't want to be accused of killing Reverend Tull and making it look like a suicide.

We walked back to the house and told my parents and sister what we'd found.

Then we called the deputy sheriff who lived in Meadowlark.

1957

Ethan and I rode the tractor to our cabin and waited for the sheriff's employees to arrive. After they did, the deputy sheriff who lived in Meadowlark explained to them who we were.

We watched them take down Ethan's father and gather evidence of his suicide. They took pictures of the stepladder and the rope.

The sheriff arrived and, with the Meadowlark deputy at his side, approached us and introduced himself.

I knew who he was. He'd led the Taft Republicans to an overwhelming victory in the county in the primary election in 1952. That summer he'd gone to the Republican convention in Chicago as a fiercely contentious and outspoken delegate for Taft.

"Which of you is Ethan Tull?" he asked.

"I am," Ethan said.

The sheriff turned to me. "And you are?"

"Reed Hauser," I said. "My family are the tenants on this property. My father and mother are Ben and Annette Hauser. Our house is on the other side of the creek."

78

"I understand the two of you found Reverend Tull here."

"We did," Ethan said.

The sheriff nodded toward the tree. "Was he hanging by his neck from that tree then as my people found him when they arrived here?"

"Yes, he was," Ethan said. "We were careful not to touch anything."

"That's right." I said.

The sheriff turned to me and nodded toward the cabin. "Is that your family's cabin?"

"It is," I said.

"Did the dead man have access to it?"

"No," I said. "The door was locked when we got here and found Ethan's father. It's still locked. I have a key and can let you in. Ethan and I sometimes do our homework in it."

The Meadowlark deputy turned to the sheriff. "They're seniors in the Meadowlark High School. My son is their classmate. He tells me they're his friends."

The deputy's son was the starting quarterback for the Fighting Larks.

The sheriff shook his head. "We won't need to look inside the cabin."

That was the end of our interrogation. The sheriff and deputy walked away.

The deputy, though, soon came back to us. He held a paper in his gloved hand. "We found this lying on the front seat of the car," he said. "You can read it, but you can't touch it."

It was a sheet of Reverend Tull's offical stationary identifying him as the pastor of the Meadowlark Church.

Ethan had told me his father had paid for it himself. The members of the board hadn't thought it was necessary for a minister of their church to have official stationary.

Ethan nodded. "It's my father's handwriting. It's his signature too."

Reverend Tull had scrawled two sentences above his signature. "The evil of this world is too much for me. I've asked Jesus to have mercy on me and take me to Heaven, to live there forever with Him."

1957

After the sheriff and his employees left, Ethan and I kept staring at the tree we'd found his father hanging from.

Ethan broke the silence. "My father knew *we'd* find him here. Our love for one another was the worst thing in his life."

"It needn't have been."

"Whether we want to admit it or not, we killed that man. He knew what we were doing. We killed him."

I shook my head. "We didn't kick over that stepladder. He did."

1957

The Sunday newscasts led with and the newspapers headlined the suicide by hanging of the former pastor of the Meadowlark Church.

The sheriff had said his people had found a suicide note in his car. Reverend Isaac Tull's handwriting and signature on the note had been confirmed.

The sheriff had chosen not to disclose the location of the suicide scene except to say Isaac Tull's body had been found hanging from the limb of a tree in a wooded area in Meadowlark Township.

The sheriff had also chosen not to disclose the identity of the person or persons who'd found the body or confirmed Tull's authorship of the note. The sheriff did reveal the precise wording Tull had chosen for his note.

The newscasts and newspapers reminded their viewers and readers Isaac Tull, 41 years old, had been convicted the previous Monday for committing homosexual activities in the men's room of a truckstop. He'd been sentenced to a year in a state prison.

Moonshine Cabin

The media said Reverend Tull was survived by a son, without disclosing either the son's name or his age. Ethan and I assumed neither the sheriff nor the Meadowlark Church would give out that information. We conceded it was possible, though, the media knew his name and age but had chosen not to invade his privacy.

Two weeks later, the newscasts and the newspapers closed the sad story. Nobody had claimed Reverend Tull's body. The authorities had therefore given him a pauper's burial.

For most of the people living in or near Meadowlark Township, I assumed, Isaac Tull's story wasn't complicated. He was a queer who'd hoodwinked a rural community into believing he was a Christian worthy of being the minister of their church. After he was convicted of committing homosexual activities in a truckstop men's room and sentenced to a year in prison, he committed suicide. What other choice did he have?

There was no need to search for other queers in hiding in the area. It was far more convenient to pretend such creatures were too rare to bother with.

And if that was how the people in our community viewed the matter, Ethan and I could only be pleased. They'd leave us alone.

1957

Marilyn and the deputy's son were dating.

The previous autumn he and the starting tight end had won the conference championship game. The Fighting Larks were three points behind but had the ball on their opponent's 35-yard line for the last play of the game. The deputy's son threw a Hail Mary into the end zone.

Like a pole vaulter but without a pole, the starting tight end rose above the three defenders surrounding him, caught the ball and brought it down with his arms wrapped around it as if it were a precious gift.

Marilyn, Ethan and I had arrived early for the game and taken seats in the first row of the grandstand behind the bench for the Fighting Larks. We loudly cheered them on.

The quarterback and tight end had decided to go to the recently renamed Northern Illinois University in DeKalb in the fall. They'd determined it would be their best chance to play for a college team.

Marilyn told us she was considering attending Northern herself. She'd graduate from high school in 1958.

1957

Ethan and I were also prepared for the future. We'd graduate from Meadowlark High School at the end of May.

Ethan's mother had agreed Ethan should continue to live with my family throughout the coming summer and every summer we were in college. During those summers, she'd sing with him every Sunday at the Meadowlark Church. She and Ethan's grandmother would be welcome to share our noon meal on Sunday whenever they wished.

Ethan and I, in our white tee shirts and blue Levi's jeans, would hire ourselves out—as much as we could and still get the work done on my family's farm—to neighboring farmers to help with their hay baling, silage making, oats harvesting and whatever other summer work they might have for us to do.

The University of Illinois had accepted our applications and offered us the scholarships we'd hoped for. During the school year we'd live in a double room in one of the university-owned dormitories. Both of us had jobs waiting for us in the cafeteria for the residents in the dormitories. We wouldn't need to ask our parents for financial assistance.

Visitors to our room would likely wonder why we'd pushed together the two single beds so they were side by side with no space between them. We'd gladly let people wonder all they wanted.

Moonshine Cabin

We'd be working ourselves through college. We'd have no obligation to explain to anybody why we lived the way we did.

We hadn't decided yet what we'd do after we graduated from college. We had no doubt, though, whatever we did in our lives, we'd be together.

www.ingramcontent.com/pod-product-compliance
Lightning Source LLC
Chambersburg PA
CBHW072041170626
46811CB00008B/3125